SIMPLE NUMEROLOGY

S I M P L E

NUMEROLOGY

Damian Sharp

CONARI PRESS
Berkeley, California

Conari Press books are distributed by Publishers Group West.

Book and cover design: Claudia Smelser
Cover illustration: The Metropolitan Museum of Art, Gift of Herbert N. Straus, 1925. Photograph © 1984 The Metropolitan Museum of Art

LIBRARY OF CONGRESS CATALOGING-IN-PUBLICATION DATA
Sharp, Damian
   Simple numerology / Damian Sharp.
      p.   cm. — (A simple wisdom book series)
   ISBN: 1–57324–560–7 (alk. paper)
   1. Numerology I. Title II. Series
BF1623.P9 S46 2001
133.3'35—dc21   2001000644

Printed in the United States of America on recycled paper

01 02 03 04 05 PHOENIX 10 9 8 7 6 5 4 3 2 1

SIMPLE NUMEROLOGY

INTRODUCTION
TO SIMPLE NUMEROLOGY

Numerology is a science of symbol, cycle, and vibration that has roots in the ancient Hindu teachings of India and in the cultures of Sumer, Egypt, Chaldea, and Phoenicia. It is found in the symbology of the Bible and the Jewish Kabbalah. Numerology provides us with a means of understanding our own individual cyclical patterns and personal qualities. Its application can be invaluable in helping us understand who we are and in helping us harmonize with the natural flow of our lives, so that we can become masters of our fate rather than its hapless victims.

This book is a basic introduction to Western or Pythagorean numerology. The serious student is encouraged to pursue further reading on this arcane, broad, and intricate subject, the scope of which is indeed immense. A list of books that provide additional information appears in Further Reading, page 123.

The Greek philosopher Pythagoras of Samos (c. 582–c. 507 B.C.E.) is the father of numerology as we know it in the West today. He was both a man of science and a teacher of mystical doctrine. Little is known of Pythagoras' life, and nothing exists firsthand of his writings. All the knowledge we have of him comes from his followers, the Pythagoreans, a mystical cult or brotherhood founded by Pythagoras at Crotone in southern Italy. Their society was both a religious community and a scientific school. His followers regarded Pythagoras as a demigod and attributed all their doctrines to him.

The Pythagoreans believed in reincarnation and the transmigration of the soul, beliefs that may have developed in the Orphic cults of the time, which came to Greece from the East and which the Greeks brought with them to their colonies in Sicily, southern Italy, and elsewhere. The Pythagoreans adhered to strict moral codes and dietary practices aimed at purifying the soul for its next physical incarnation. They were skilled mathematicians, and their theories and discoveries influenced early Euclidean geometry. They were among the first to teach that the Earth is a spherical body that revolves around a fixed point.

Pythagoras argued that there were three kinds of people, just as there were three classes of strangers who came to the Olympic Games. The lowest class consisted of those who came to buy and sell. Above them were those who came to compete. The highest were those who came simply to look on. In Pythagoras's view, people could accordingly be classified as lovers of gain, lovers of honor, and lovers of wisdom, implying the doctrine of the tripartite soul.

One of Pythagoras' great contributions to philosophy is the theory that what gives form to the "Unlimited" is the "Limited." The function of the limit was best expressed for the Pythagoreans in music and medicine, and ultimately in Pythagoras' theory that all things were numbers.

Pythagoras' theory of numbers began with the discovery of numerical relations between numbers and musical notes. Hence, in numerology, numbers are tied to tones or vibrations. Pythagoras taught that at the core of all things, including people and even abstract notions such as justice and equality, were numbers: things and relationships could be expressed numerically. The science of numbers as it is today, as well as the meanings attributed to them by numerology, is part of Pythagoras' remarkable legacy.

HOW TO FIND YOUR NUMBERS

The anthropogeny of the numbers one to nine in numerology is derived from two sources: your name and your date of birth. Like astrology, numerology represents the soul's and the personality's journey through evolution, what some astrologers and philosophers refer to as "the process of individuation on the Wheel of Life," from the birth of the first awareness of self, to the awareness of, union with, and begetting of other, to the awareness of society and eventually the cosmos and the invisible forces that govern it. There are thus direct correlations between astrology and numerology; for example, between the astrological sign Aries and the number one, at the beginning of the cycle, and Pisces and the number nine at the end. As you will see, the corresponding meanings of astrological signs and numbers will be actually manifested in an individual's astrological chart and numerological birthpath number.

YOUR NAME NUMBER

Your name number reveals your outer nature, the personality

that cloaks the inner you and that you present to the outer world. Finding your name number is quite simple.

Using your complete name as written on your birth certificate, refer to the table following and the number assigned to each of the letters in the alphabet. Each letter is assigned a number one through nine, based on the ancient Pythagorean system.

1	2	3	4	5	6	7	8	9
A	B	C	D	E	F	G	H	I
J	K	L	M	N	O	P	Q	R
S	T	U	V	W	X	Y	Z	

Add together all of the letters of your full birth name and reduce the total number to a single digit.

Example

Kelly	Nicole	Harrison
$2+5+3+3+7=20$	$5+9+3+6+3+5=31$	$8+1+9+9+9+1+6+5=48$

$20 + 31 + 48 = 99$

$9 + 9 = 18$

$1 + 8 = 9$

Kelly Nicole Harrison's name number is 9.

As explained in a later chapter, there are three numbers, called Master Numbers, which do not reduce to a single number. The Master Numbers are 11, 22, and 33. They are considered to have special vibrations related to their single-digit totals of 2, 4, and 6, respectively (1 + 1, 2 + 2, and 3 + 3), but they remain double-digit numbers in all calculations. If in your calculations of your birth name you arrive at a final number of 11, 22, or 33, do not combine those numbers for a final total but, instead, consider the Master Number to be your number.

Many numerologists believe that the Pythagorean system (or Western system) can be only applied to names that are based on the Western alphabet. However, in our increasingly multicultural society, this opinion is now open to question; for example, people of Chinese descent have taken Western first names or write their Chinese names in English. In numerological terms this changes, or adds to, the meaning and vibration of the name, in the same way that a married woman who takes her husband's surname changes her number from that of her original birth name. Changing your name in any way will change its number and, therefore, certain aspects of your personality and destiny.

The number derived from your full birth name describes your outer expression while also revealing your essential being. It will always be a major influence despite any nickname or name change you might use.

For the meanings attached to your specific birth name number, see the individual chapters in the next part of the book, "The Numbers and Their Meanings."

Often, the name number and birthpath number share similar characteristics, with the birthpath number an elaboration of the name number. Your birthpath number represents those traits and talents, often hidden, that you are yearning to develop and reveal. This is the number that reveals your inner nature and your purpose in life. The attributes inherent in this number will by honed and polished by experience. The birthpath number is found by adding together the month, day, and year of your birth, and then reducing that figure to a single digit. Be sure to total all four digits in the year (for example, 1958, not '58).

Example

If Octavio's birthday is June 16, 1960, his birthpath number is calculated as follows:

6/16/1960
6 + 1 + 6 + 1 + 9 + 6 + 0 = 29
2 + 9 = 11

As noted before, the master numbers 11, 22, and 33 are not re-duced to a single digit. So, Octavio's birthpath number is 11.

In conclusion, you can see that you have two numbers: a name number and a birthpath number. Your name number describes the persona that you present to the outer world, the form, as it were, that you take. Your birthpath number represents both your destiny and the inner you, the content that underlies the outer image presented by your name number.

THE NUMBERS

AND

THEIR MEANINGS

WILL: INDIVIDUALITY

The Number One Name Number

One is the number of the self, of individuality, will, independence, and originality. The number one personality expresses leadership and pioneering efforts and the promotion of fortitude and honesty, sometimes to the point of being too blunt and frank. Ones can be strong willed and ambitious, courageous leaders and original thinkers. They are prone to self-centeredness and a desire to be first in all things—literally, Number One. They can be very demanding as well as commanding, are often extremely witty and charming, and are very regal and dignified. They hide their insecurities behind a brash and assertive manner, while at the same time maintaining an aura of personal mystery and secretiveness. They can sometimes appear to be stupidly selfish, putting their own needs and desires before others regardless of personal consequences. In such cases, one can note that the Greek root for the word *idiot* means "a man alone." When in this negative mode, ones seldom listen to others, but they love to give directions. When things do not easily go their way, they can become passive, dependent, stubborn, and procrastinating, fearful of making decisions or showing initiative. Ones need to find the balance between their own extremes. One is a masculine number, and in a woman suggests a strong *animus* (male spirit).

In relationships, it is best for a one to seek a spouse or companion who is strong willed and assertive but supportive and patient. Despite all of their braggadocio about self-reliance and individuality, ones fare best within the security of a steady and stable relationship. They need affection and attention and are capable of giving totally to their mates. They approach love and romance with a straightforward intensity, with little time for small talk and subtlety. Their emotions are stronger than they would like to admit (out of a fear of vulnerability and exposure), but attraction and loyalty are the key components to their relationships. When romantic difficulties arise, ones can be prone to sudden fits of temper, caustic bluntness, and silent withdrawal, and can become irritating martinets over such issues as cleanliness, rules, and their own capricious whims. However, they recover quickly and do not harbor grudges, expecting to be forgiven as they themselves forgive, or forget. When their balance is upset, they can be stubborn, tyrannical, domineering, and even harsh and brutal to those involved with them. They can be emotionally fickle and unreliable, and inclined to dominate and manipulate others' feelings. They can be afraid to engage in emotional relationships, have great difficulties trusting their own feelings, be demanding of attention while refusing to give any back in return, and have a strong need to win an argument merely for the sake of their egos.

In terms of careers or employment, ones fair best when they have the freedom to be independent and original. It is difficult for them to take orders, and they are generally better off working for themselves. Designer, entertainer, artist, explorer, inventor, manager, and athlete are all professions suited to people with the name number one.

Typically, ones are robust, energetic, and healthy. They are, however, inclined to overestimate their own limits and can jeopardize their health through overwork and lack of rest. Ones are often prone to headaches and arthritis.

The Number One Birthpath Number

People with the number one birthpath number are natural-born leaders and pioneers, fearless, adventurous, and driven by their own morals and convictions. They are full of initiative and absolutely compelled to forge ahead. They have been born into this world to learn individuality, self-reliance, and the proper expression of will, the *I am*. More than likely, they have had to deal with a dominating, interfering, or unyielding parent in childhood, which created early tension and conflict between parent and child. The resulting resentment explodes in their late teens or early twenties and a period of rebellion follows, as ones, in order to assert their self-identity, refuse to take orders or advice from others, especially spouses or partners. During this rebellious stage, their stubbornness, assertiveness, isolation, and selfishness can be extremely irritating and, for them personally, myopic and self-defeating. Ones need to learn that pure rebellion and reaction do not necessarily lead to independence and self-fulfillment.

Quite likely, their sense of adventure and enterprise could remain dormant or unrealized in their early years, with them believing that they most desire stability, security, and comfort. Early marriages, therefore, are ill advised for those with the number one birthpath, who, with their impatient and courageous spirits, are also inclined to act impulsively and not look before they leap.

Challenge, accomplishment, and action are the *modus operandi* of the number one birthpath. They are, indeed, constantly out to prove themselves. Challenges will be met and overcome for the sheer sake of proving the one could do it. Once success has been achieved, however, the number one is prone to walk away, seeking new fields to conquer. On the negative side, when feeling less confident, ones can be guilty of procrastination, concocting any number of seemingly logical and realistic excuses why a challenge should not or can not be met. This never lasts for very long. Inevitably, life itself will compel the number one to take some form of action, whether chosen or not. Ernest Hemingway had a one birthpath number. He was a pioneer and innovator, creating a modern literary style and vision that was concerned with individuality, courage, and masculine expression through a declaratory, albeit blunt, prose style. All of these elements, including the need constantly to meet a challenge, test, and prove himself, were also reflected in his life. They were both his strength and his weakness. His full birth name, Ernest Miller Hemingway, makes his name number a three, the number of self-expression and creativity (see the chapter on number three).

PEACE: COOPERATION

The Number Two Name Number

The lesson of the number two is primarily that of coopera-tion and peace, of the development of the awareness of Other beyond the Self. As a result, twos are diplomatic, tactful, and persuasive, and are good listeners, able to mediate between conflicting parties and bring about harmonious resolutions. Masters of the art of persuasion, they are able to accumulate and quote facts and figures accurately to enhance their bargain-ing positions. When negative, this ability can be used to manip-ulate and distort information to win an argument or support an opinion. When thwarted or blocked, twos can be cunning and scheming in order to get what they desire. Also, they can be-come too involved in the minor and petty details of things like dress, work, or manners in order to impress others; they can come across as contrived and hypocritical.

They are very astute at working behind the scenes to accom-plish their goals. Highly adaptable and flexible, twos cope well in a wide variety of circumstances and with people from diverse social, ethnic, religious, and political backgrounds.

Twos are likely to have encountered considerable criticism and conflict in early childhood, making them extremely sensitive to tension, discord, and strife in any form. They are highly gregarious creatures and thrive in the company of others, but can be hurt deeply if they are misunderstood or rejected. They can harbor a deep unconscious fear of other people's reactions to them, making them overly self-conscious. It is important that they realize and confront this fear and rid themselves of it.

Twos operate on the belief that good will always triumph over evil. This attitude, coupled with their innate charm, enables them to attract the people they need to get things done. Partnership and team effort are important to twos. They find their strength in roles that support and enhance leadership rather than in leadership itself. This does not mean that they lack ambition or the drive to reach the top, only that the ambition expresses itself in a subtle, cooperative, and harmonious way. Typically, twos are found in careers and professions pertaining to politics, public relations, technology, and religion. Two is a feminine number, and in a man suggests a strong *anima* (feminine spirit).

With their strong need for understanding and discomfort with being alone, twos fare best when in steady relationships or marriages. They are likely to choose as a spouse someone quiet, reserved, and supportive, who is clean and orderly around the home. In romance, details pertaining to both partner and environment are very important. For a two, such things as small flaws in a partner's body, a cluttered kitchen sink, or a dripping tap can ruin the pleasure of the moment.

Twos have a strong penchant for critical speech, which psychologically and physically makes them prone to sore throats, tonsillitis, and thyroid conditions. The number two is related to the brain and nervous system, and with their sensitivity to conflict and strife twos can be susceptible to nervous disorders.

The Number Two Birthpath Number

Like people with the number two name number, those with the two birthpath are often born into families where a parent or parents are inclined to pettiness and negative criticism. The number two child is rarely complimented or given positive reinforcement for his or her efforts or accomplishments, but is more often reminded that whatever has been achieved isn't good enough. Such an environment can serve to undermine the two's self-confidence and ability to cope with criticism later in life. As a result, a two may find it hard to make a decision out of fear of being wrong.

Often, those with a two birthpath number are targets of unwarranted criticism and gossip, especially in adolescence and the early years of adulthood. It is important for twos to learn not to respond negatively to these attacks, but rather to shed themselves of judgmental and critical attitudes in themselves.

Twos are natural diplomats who are able to achieve their

goals through gentle persuasion and tact rather than force. More often than not, they are found in the middle ranks of their chosen careers. When a two does reach a position of leadership, it is always through diplomacy, influence, and finesse. They are at their best when working with a team rather than in solitude, and are expert at uniting divergent groups or people in a cooperative effort. Often, twos are the ones doing the real work behind the scenes for those who publicly receive the glory. When balanced, twos are calm, patient, and poised, always willing to consider varying points of view, expert at intuitively evaluating people and situations and making fair and accurate judgments. In their negative modes, twos can become caught up in trivial details, use distorted logic, and become stubborn, unyielding, and intolerant.

Virgo, Libra, and Scorpio tend to be prominent in the natal horoscopes of people who have the number two birthpath.

CREATIVITY: SELF-EXPRESSION

The Number Three Name Number

Three is the number of creativity, beauty, joy, and self-expression. Threes work in the realm of the creative imagination; as a result, they can be prone to vivid elaboration and exaggeration in conversation, having little time or patience for the prosaic and mundane. They are blessed with optimistic dispositions and are generally cheerful and highly sociable. Threes value friendship and are good and loyal friends. They are particularly comfortable with potential lovers and, being perpetual romantics, are often involved in adventurous affairs.

Threes embrace the good life and all it has to offer. They enjoy luxury and lavish surroundings. If they give luxury, ease, and self-indulgence priority over creative expression, they can become shallow, egocentric, contrived, and superficial. Gifted with natural eloquence and wit, threes can be highly entertaining, informative, and fascinating. Their lives are a maze of colorful and intriguing experiences, making them marvelous raconteurs. They also tend to have lovely voices. When negative, they can talk too much while saying very little, be scattered and undisciplined, oversexed, confused by emotional issues, unable to bring their imaginative ideas to practical fruition, and have decidedly gaudy taste in dress and decorum.

In romance, emotional harmony is particularly important to them, and they are deeply affectionate and capable of giving to the point of self-sacrifice. A three will prefer a spouse or partner who is dedicated, strong, and responsible, someone who will appreciate his enthusiastic and vivid imagination and world-view while complementing him with a sense of practicality and realism.

Threes are quite naturally attracted to careers in the arts, media, entertainment, law, education, social work, travel, and the clergy—any career that provides an outlet for their imagination and self-expression. Audrey Hepburn, whose full name was Audrey Ralston Hepburn, was a three.

In health matters, the number three is related to the voice and sexual organs, both symbolic of creative functions. When creative functions are blocked, or there is emotional imbalance and disturbance, sexual guilt, or confusion, these organs, along with the kidneys, are prone to ailments. Threes have strong intuitive and psychic abilities and can be inspired in speech and art, but in order for them to receive and channel these impulses it is important that sexual guilt be overcome.

The Number Three Birthpath Number

Where the number one birthpath number represents aggressive

male or yang energy (the primal assertion of the self), and the number two female or yin energy (that which is intuitive and nurturing), the number three is the product of the union of these two and represents the form and function of creative self-expression. In archetypal terms it is the number of the word spoken, the avatar, the manifestation of creative consciousness and bringer of the universal message. When threes are in balance and harmony, the manifestation of their creative abilities and the opportunities to express them flow naturally. However, threes are often born into families in which their creative gifts are met with considerable resistance, repression, hostility, or indifference—the obstacles that threes must overcome.

Sexuality—libido—is an intrinsic aspect of the creative force. The same creative energy that is expressed in the physical act of sexual intercourse is channeled into other forms of creative expression. Feelings of sexual guilt, shame, or embarrassment that can come as a result of early childhood experiences and repression can leave a subconscious scar that inhibits the creative process in later life. Threes so afflicted may be prone to self-sabotage in their creative endeavors, scattering their energies by starting several projects at once and failing to complete or excel in any of them, or prematurely terminating a project in midstream. It is of absolute necessity that threes recognize and come to terms with this internal conflict. Once the struggle is won, life can be glorious for a three. At their very best, they are inspired, imaginative, and able to plumb the deepest recesses of emotion, intuition, and collective consciousness. They make excellent hosts, and benefit greatly from the company of other creative seekers and doers. However, they must always be careful that they do not waste their innate talents in self-indulgence, luxury, and facile dilettantism or pretentiousness.

When three appears as the birthpath number, Libra or Sagittarius is often prominent in the natal horoscope.

WORK: DISCIPLINE

The Number Four Name Number

A person with the number four name number is characteristically loyal, honest, dedicated, and hard working. They are reliable, steady, and methodical, and strive to build solid foundations in their homes, businesses, and communities. Preferring work to socializing, they do not give themselves over easily to life's pleasures. They can be rigid and fixed in their attitudes and habits, and thus risk confining themselves to a narrow rut. The early childhood of a four often takes place in an environment in which there is an overemphasis on hard work. Fours can be inclined to be tight with their money and possessions and to see hardship where none actually exists.

Fours are generally conservative. Hard work, thrift, prudence, and orderliness are the virtues they most admire and adhere to, and they are often intolerant, resentful, or even hostile toward people whom they perceive as not pulling their own weight or not willing to earn their own way in life. Fours take pride in their work, and their self-image is based upon their accomplishments, property, and social standing. Imagination is not a great strength or resource. They like routine and get ahead in life on practicality, organization, technical skill, and industriousness. They are not inclined to take risks that might in any way jeopardize their solid sense of security.

If fours feel confined or boxed in, they are usually the people responsible for that condition. However, when harshly restricted by circumstance, they are not shy about giving voice to their discontent. Their resentment builds slowly and then explodes. When they are unhappy with their work or its rewards, or feel that the work is beneath their dignity, those around them will suffer, and fours can become extremely resentful toward those who seem to be getting more than they deserve.

At times, their hesitant conservatism, caution, and dislike of speculation can cause them to miss opportunities and then become bitter at their own misfortune—or, more appropriately, lack of luck—and jealous of those who were willing to take the risk and were consequently successful.

As bosses, fours tend to be harsh and demanding. They are inclined to overwork themselves and expect others to do the same. When negative, they can overestimate their own abilities to compensate for a poor self-image, take their work too seriously, and be overly concerned with fixed procedures. When harmonious, fours are extremely loyal, patient, capable, dependable, thorough, and economical.

Spontaneous enjoyment, mixing with others, and indulging

in small talk can be very difficult for a four. Their fixed attitudes and opinions can make them intolerant, prejudiced, and judgmental of others. When challenged or confronted with an opinion that threatens their foundation, they can feel defenseless and vulnerable—as though the ground was falling out from beneath their feet—and become aggressively argumentative, stubborn, and overly defensive, often refusing to change their minds even when they have been proved wrong.

In romance fours are ardent but contained. They can be uncomfortable and insecure in emotional relationships unless they feel they are in control. This can make them domineering, unyielding, and possessive. They are loyal and steadfast, and require the same in return. They are very proud and protective of their loved ones and very generous and warmhearted toward their families.

Craftwork, building, chemistry, electronics, accounting, farming, science, banking, the police, and the military are all professions and careers suited to the four personality.

Hardening of the arteries, tendonitis, bone disorders, backaches, male baldness, and neuralgia are all health problems associated with the number four.

The Number Four Birthpath Number

The number four is represented by the square, the symbol of the

Earth. Four is the number of hard work. It is the number of the plowman and the builder, of humanity sent forth from Eden to establish itself firmly upon the Earth. It is the fate of those born with the four birthpath number to strive with dedication and diligence toward their goals, for theirs is the burden of labor. Things generally do not come easily to them, but only through effort. When a four attains a position of wealth, it is through hard work and persistence. The stubborn diligence of the number four can also make them good at overcoming others' negativity.

Fours are loyal, intense, and devoted workers. However, they can show a considerable lack of imagination, originality, or ability to improvise when called upon to make adjustments that may be required by changes in conditions or circumstances. Fours need to be shown the practical and tangible side of things before they can grasp new ideas or begin new projects. They naturally gravitate toward engineering, mechanical, and technical fields, and administration. They are inclined to be conservative and protective, and must have a clear knowledge of all the facts before they'll take any risks. In short, they need to see it to believe it. They may experience a variety of jobs or occupations before settling into a position that suits them.

Fours have a highly developed sense of their own self-worth and dignity. They will be helpful to those in need, but their rigid and conservative natures tend to limit their friends and associates. As employers or supervisors, they expect complete dedication from their employees and can be guilty of being stringent and overbearing.

When four is the birthpath number, Taurus or Capricorn will tend to be prominent in the natal horoscope.

five

FREEDOM: CHANGE

The Number Five Name Number

Fives are decidedly marked by their aura of adventure, restlessness, curiosity, sensuality, and freedom. They have strong sexual magnetism and are very physically attractive. They are characteristically carefree, witty, and enthusiastic, with a love of travel and meeting new people. They are hungry for life's experiences, crave change and excitement, and deplore the monotonous and prosaic. They are fascinated by the events and people around them, and are eager to joyously participate. This attitude is generally wholesome, progressive, adaptable, independent, and growth oriented, but can lead to careless disregard for legal and moral codes, with a tendency to seek escape through overindulgence in sensory stimulation through sex, drugs, alcohol, or food.

Five is the number of the wanderer and adventurer, and it is difficult for a five to stay attached to people or places for any significant length of time. They see life as a gamble, and find its meaning in taking chances. They can become critical and impatient with slow-moving situations or delays. When insecure or emotionally or psychologically arrested, they repeat the same experience again and again, trapped in a cycle of behavior but failing to learn from the experience itself and move on.

Fives are very adroit with words and ideas and are able to mingle and blend with a wide variety of people and groups. They very much enjoy the company of others and are likely to have many friends of both sexes.

In romance, they are flirtatious, fickle, and invariably highly entertaining. They prefer a variety of sexual partners, in keeping with their wanderlust and hunger for new experiences of every kind. It is indeed difficult to tie a five down, but they have a lot to give and are very giving while they're around.

In marriage, the five naturally requires a lot of freedom and latitude. A five is happiest with a mate who is independent, adventurous, active, and versatile, and who can keep her curious and intrigued enough to want to stay around—or accompany her on her ongoing journey. Athletic and outdoor activities are important to the five's physical as well as emotional well-being. They find it hard to adapt to the constraints and demands of family life, but if content with their mates can be colorful, entertaining, and loving companions. The best mate for a five is someone capable of being both friend and lover.

Vocations best suited to the number five include entertainment fields of all descriptions: acting, writing, directing films, photography, journalism, along with travel consulting, sales, exploring, and sports.

Health matters related to the number five include problems with the senses (eyes, ears, nose, skin). Problems with the liver, kidneys, and intestines can arise as a result of overindulgence, and nervous ailments can be caused by overactivity.

The Number Five Birthpath Number

Five is the number of free will, the mind, and the five senses. The number five was born into this life to experience all of Earth's offerings, and the path of the senses is the path to knowledge. Embracing Pythagoras' theories of numerology and reincarnation, the five's previous life was one of abstinence, asceticism, and possibly impoverishment, in which contact with mundane and human desires was sedulously avoided. Now, the five has returned as a seeker of earthly experience, and the five finds herself torn between strong physical urges and desires and the dictates and restrictions of religion, morals, and social mores. Their lives tend to fluctuate between these two extremes in dealing with desire—between saint and sinner, or vice versa. Saint Augustine, in his *Confessions,* comes across as a prototypical five: "Oh Lord, give me the strength, but not yet."

Having come from a previous life of monastic seclusion and self-denial and hungry for the world, fives now seek the proper balance within the self and the correct expression of their sensual and sexual needs and desires. The esoteric knowledge of the number five is that of the duality of existence, of free will and natural law. The lesson of the number five lies in finding the course of correct action and the balance between the needs and desires of the body and those of the soul.

Fives benefit and learn most from contact with other people; they have much to learn and are eager students. One of their purposes in life is to tolerate no old prejudices. They will have the chance to mingle with all types of humanity—the rich, the poor, people of different races, creeds, and cultures. Quite often, you will find fives involved in interracial marriages and relationships.

When negative and shallow, fives can try a little of everything but learn nothing. They become superficial and unable to commit to a sustained relationship. On the other extreme, they can become so overwhelmed in their involvement in an experience or relationship that they are unable to break from it and try new opportunities. A five strives to attain the balance of knowing when he or she has learned from an experience and needs to move on. When imbalanced or blocked, a five will seek excitement and stimulation in sexual excess, drink, drugs, and other sensual indulgences.

When five occurs as the birthpath number, often Gemini or Leo is prominent in the natal horoscope.

SERVICE: RESPONSIBILITY

The Number Six Name Number

Six is the number of service, responsibility, domesticity, and emotional harmony. Sixes are sympathetic and considerate. Their thoughts are naturally concerned with others and the needs of those close to them, and they themselves are possessed of a strong need to serve and assist. They are highly empathetic, and when positive are able to aid and support their friends and associates through troubled times. On the negative side, their abilities as empaths can be used to manipulate and coerce others by tapping into their fears and insecurities. Winston Churchill, whose full birth name was Winston Leonard Spencer Churchill, is a six name number.

Sixes tend to be highly sensitive to any negative thoughts and feelings around them, making them susceptible to dark moods and feelings of discouragement, anxiety, and insecurity. They are capable of deep affection and self-sacrifice, but can be prone to angry outbursts of righteous indignation when they feel that their loved ones are not responding with the loyalty, affection, or concern they believe they deserve. They can be champions of lost causes, pursuing their lofty purposes with quixotic zeal. A feeling of duty to others is intrinsic to their natures, but it is important that sixes learn to help others without allowing those they are assisting to drain them of their own energies. There are those who will see the six's desire to serve as a weakness.

They have strong, heartfelt convictions about right and wrong and are adamant about issues concerned with justice and equality. They can take offense when misunderstood, and can easily dismay others with demonstrations of hurt and pettiness over trivial matters.

Naturally, they place a high value on friendship and find great joy and nourishment in the company of others. They can, however, be prone to believing they know what is best for another's well-being and can be overbearing and interfering in their concern.

In romance, they are sentimental, idealistic, protective, and considerate. Emotional harmony is very important as a precursor to sexual union and enjoyment. When the relationship is in doubt or jeopardy of any sort they can become jealous and possessive, often irrationally so. Rejection can be very painful for them.

Sixes are good providers who lavish their loved ones with luxury and affection; they are extremely well suited to domestic life. In fact, domestic security and harmony are necessary for them to operate successfully in their chosen fields. However, domestic bliss and stability may not come to them until after more than one marriage.

Professions best suited to the six include doctor, nurse, teacher, counselor, artist, and musician.

Sixes can be prone to stomach disorders as a result of excessive worries and anxieties. Heart and gall bladder ailments can occur as a result of rejection.

The Number Six Birthpath Number

Sixes are born into a life of service, responsibility, and domesticity. Their greatest personal challenge is to establish emotional balance and security. Often, they are born into families that are plagued by discord and opposition between the parents and result in divorce, leaving a deep unconscious feeling of insecurity in the number six child.

Those with the six birthpath number often have difficulty adjusting to the responsibilities of home and family. There is often more than one marriage in their lives before they learn to live in harmonious balance with their mates. They will have to work hard to find tranquility and happiness in married life—this is a part of the lesson of the six—but once found, contentment, harmony, and security can be firmly established.

Sixes have come into this life to be of service to others, and are at their best when their work benefits others rather than working in the more competitive professions. They are here to serve the greater cause of self-sacrifice for humanity. Their skill as empaths makes them natural healers of the mind, body, and soul. Doctors, nurses, ministers, teachers, social workers, psychologists, and counselors are often sixes. A six's idealism and altruism can create very strong opinions as to what is best for others, and they should be wary of people taking advantage of their generosity as well as of interfering where they are not wanted.

With the number six birthpath, Cancer or Pisces is usually prominent in the natal horoscope.

WISDOM: DETACHMENT

The Number Seven Name Number

The number seven is a born seeker of truth. Wisdom, detachment, intellectualism, and skepticism are hallmarks of the seven personality. The seven emits a strong aura of self-knowledge. In Pythagorean terms, their wisdom comes from all that they have been in their past lives. They are deep thinkers and can express their beliefs with force and courage. They are cerebral, logical, opinionated, and honest, and it is very difficult to persuade them to deviate from their asserted position, as it as been arrived at after much acute observation and informed contemplation. Leonardo da Vinci is a seven name number.

Their originality can be found in their thought processes and suppositions. If they become overly intellectual, practical matters may be entirely overlooked, which can greatly hamper their success in business affairs. In personal relationships, they often appear as detached or even indifferent.

They enjoy delving into the mysteries of life, death, creation, and the universe, and will investigate almost anything that captures their interest and attention. Highly scientific in their approach, they can overestimate the value of mental knowledge and become arrogant and intellectual. On the other hand, they are capable of bringing great wisdom and profound truths to light when intuition is balanced with intellectual prowess, reason, and knowledge.

Sevens tend to be dignified and poised in public. They dislike large gatherings and raucous parties, as their own emphasis on discipline and mental endeavors prevents them from enjoying life's superficialities and frivolities. When discussing topics in which they are knowledgeable they are convincing and eloquently at ease; however, when uninformed they can make impulsive statements that they later regret.

They are very private individuals who dislike divulging personal information, yet greatly enjoy prying into another's personal affairs. They can be cynical and suspicious of other people's motives.

In romance, intellectual rapport with their mates is of supreme importance. Once trust has been established, they are extremely loyal and capable of deep feelings. Their love is enduring and sincere. Difficulties can arise in marriage as a result of the seven's tendency to detach emotionally and withdraw.

Sevens make excellent scientists, analysts, writers, investigators, and educators. Health matters related to the number seven include glandular, pancreas, and spleen problems, and where there is severe bitterness and cynicism, cancer.

The Number Seven Birthpath Number

Those with the seven birthpath number are in constant search of knowledge both of themselves and of the world around them. Theirs is the number of introspection, meditation, and self-examination. They analyze, investigate, and probe deep for hidden information in their ongoing quest for knowledge, a trait they apply in some regard to everything they do.

Sevens tend to lead lonely lives of introspection and detachment. Strength is found in the self, and they can find it difficult to open up to others for guidance and assistance. Because of their overemphasis on the life of the mind, they can be neglectful of personal and practical needs and unable to enjoy the seemingly trivial pleasures of social life. They prefer to wear masks of superior indifference rather than participate in anything they perceive as petty or mundane.

Their dedication and scientific approach often enables them to accomplish a great deal and attain considerable success. Sevens need to learn the balance between compassion and sensitivity and the empirical pursuit of knowledge. When awakened to inner realities, they are able to probe into the deepest mysteries of life and bring profound knowledge and understanding to light. When negative, they can be prone to excessive skepticism and destructive cynicism, indulging in false rhetoric and subterfuge. One of the lessons of the seven is to learn to integrate the intuitive heart and the rational mind, thus opening up the opportunity for immense spiritual growth and mystical understanding.

Sevens use their intellectual abilities like the sword Excalibur in Arthurian legend—a weapon for justice and truth as well as for power and control. They can intimidate with their powers of reasoning and impeccable recitation of the facts. When negative and motivated by egotism and pride, they can be cunning and deceptive.

Scorpio or Aquarius is often prominent in the natal horoscopes of people who have seven as their birthpath number.

eight

POWER: AUTHORITY

The Number Eight Name Number

Eight is the number of power, leadership, and success. People who have the eight name number are at home in the competitive world, are driven by a strong inner will, and have a distinctly independent belief in their ability to handle almost any situation. They command respect from others, leaders and subordinates alike. They tend to be conservative in their thinking and entertain strong opinions about those who act or behave contrary to their beliefs.

As natural-born leaders, eights have keen insight into what motivates and inspires others, making them excellent managers and captains of industry. It can also enable them to use others ruthlessly for personal gain. When in this negative mode, often as a result of an internal distrust of their own abilities, they can be overly suspicious of others—to the point of paranoia—and impossible to deal with on any rational basis. They can be reluctant to show tenderness or compassion out of fear that it will be judged as weakness, and can demonstrate a need to dominate every situation and relationship.

Their power and success come almost exclusively as a result of self-discipline. They are highly competitive by nature, and always on the go. Eights need to learn the importance of relaxation and the lesson that money merely for the sake of wealth and power comes at a high personal price. Money and power acquired for their own sake are worthless and destructive; true power and success come as a result of the right motivation. Once this is recognized and understood, mastery of the self and others is acquired, and the life of an eight can become a beacon of integrity, power, influence, and success.

In romance, eights prefer partners of similar drive and ambition. They will sometimes seek romance and sexual activity merely to bolster a suffering self-image. They can be mechanical in their lovemaking, certainly ardent in the moment but finishing quickly in order to get back to work. They desire spouses who are able and strong partners. Eights value and enjoy all the trappings of good living as symbols of their status and success.

Typical professions compatible with the number eight are stockbroker, corporate executive, business manager, engineer, and athlete.

Health matters related to the number eight include indigestion, ulcers, high blood pressure, and hardening of the arteries.

The Number Eight Birthpath Number

Eights have been born into the world to learn to deal with

power, authority, and leadership. Part of their lesson is to learn the proper value and utilization of money. Eights more than any other number attract money to themselves, and when wealth and esteem are their only motivation they find it slipping away from them until the primary lesson is learned and fully understood.

They are often born into families where parental authority was severely enforced or life was governed and restricted by religious, ethnic, or intellectual dogma. The tendency in youth is for eights to resent being on the lower rungs of the ladder and the victim of misused or incompetent leadership. As a result, they become determined, consciously or not, to gain their own power and authority when their time comes. Eights have an innate and uncanny ability to read another's strengths and weaknesses, and they may use this talent to manipulate others to attain purely self-centered objectives. On the other hand, using this same talent, they make excellent executives and managers. When positively motivated, eights are the great organizers and administrators, overseeing the establishment and workings of great cities, governments, and cultural and economic institutions.

Because of their innate need to appear successful, all eights seek the material symbols of success and power—opulent homes, expensive cars, whatever is important in their particular culture.

The enlightened eight is never fearful of others taking away his or her power and authority, for she has come to learn that by helping others she brings only increase to herself. Such eights have come to the full consciousness that to rule is to serve. They are at their best when executing others' dreams and visions, in which their sound leadership and executive skills can be brought to the fore. An integrated eight strives for the knowledge and understanding that enables enlightened leadership.

When eight appears as the birthpath number, Capricorn is generally prominent in the natal horoscope.

COMPASSION: ALTRUISM

The Number Nine Name Number

Nine is the number of idealism, altruism, generosity, tolerance, and sacrifice. Nines are the optimistic visionaries and dreamers whose principals inspire, guide, and shape the world. They are artistic, poetic, and mystical, and live in an inner world of ideas and ideals. They are neither practical nor materialistic, yet always manage to be provided with whatever they need. They are not at home in business unless it is an endeavor aimed at serving some greater cause for humanity.

Nines tend to think more in generalities than in details. They are emotionally very impressionable, are extremely generous, and are often easily taken advantage of. In such circumstances, it is important that they learn to forgive and not harbor feelings of bitterness and revenge. Given their sensitivity, they can be prone to dark moods and depression. They can swing from energetic states of joy and elation to melancholy and listlessness.

They will have boundless opportunities to travel and experience life firsthand. Once nines have found their purpose in life and a community to which they truly belong, their potential for service is unlimited, inspiring others through art, music, writing, or enlightened leadership.

In their many lives, nines have come through much sorrow, disappointment, illness, and loss. They know the burdens of existence and have risen above them to a greater understanding of life's higher purpose. Henry David Thoreau had a number nine name number.

In romance, nines can fall passionately in love with an ideal. Often, the reality with which they are eventually confronted is a source of deep disappointment, and they move on—another ideal mate awaits. They seek appreciation, recognition, and sympathy from a lover, and can be very loving and giving in return. Marriage can be quite difficult for them because of their idealism. Too often they are disappointed when they discover that their mate was not what they had imagined or hoped for. In love, they must learn to let go of their high ideals and accept people for who and what they are.

Vocations best suited to the nine are those of artist, writer, inventor, political or social reformer, minister, philosopher, humanitarian, and explorer.

In health matters, nines are prone to nerve and digestive disorders related directly to the extreme fluctuations of their emotions.

The Number Nine Birthpath Number

The number nine birthpath represents the final number, or end, of a major evolutionary cycle. On the metaphysical plane, nines are preparing to begin a new journey on yet another level of the cosmic spiral or wheel—as a number one with a higher realization of individuality. Subsequently, they are here to let go of the things of this world. If they do not, and insist upon worldly attachments for their security, fate will most likely remove their material wealth and force the nine to embrace the spiritual path to which he or she is preordained. The more tenaciously and fearfully a nine clings to worldly affairs—be it material possessions or even a loved one—the more intense their loss and suffering will be.

Those nines who have learned to let go and embrace their true purpose receive divine aid, and life is often a rich cornucopia. Once the need has been abolished, the world showers them with abundance, like the biblical manna from heaven. Their lives are marked by adventure, remarkable people and events, inexplicable and seemingly magical occurrences, creativity, artistic achievement, and invention.

When nine appears as the birthpath number, Aquarius and Pisces tend to be prominent in the natal horoscope.

eleven, twenty-two, and thirty-three

THE MASTER NUMBERS

The three master numbers—eleven, twenty-two, and thirty-three—are extensions of their single digit totals—two, four, and six. Those people who have master numbers as their name or birthpath numbers are generally distinguished by their special gifts of leadership and understanding.

ELEVEN: REVELATION

The Number Eleven Name Number

As an extension of the number two, eleven intensifies the desire to serve humanity and bring about peace and reconciliation. Individuals with eleven as a name number possess the added drive they need to attain positions of influence from which they can achieve their purpose. If ambition and personal gain become motivating forces, the number eleven may suffer public humiliation and repudiation. Many famous politicians, religious leaders, scholars, and entertainers have eleven prominent in their numerological charts.

The Number Eleven Birthpath Number

The eleven birthpath is similar to the two birthpath number, with some distinctions. Elevens tend to be drawn to movements and organizations that have idealistic aims, and they are likely to gain public attention and prominence. When overly zealous, they can become fanatical, and in their pursuit of the ideal become insensitive and inconsiderate, running the risk of alienating the very people upon whom they depend or wish to inspire.

When balanced, the number eleven is able to bring higher truths to bear in worldly affairs and is an innovative and visionary leader.

TWENTY-TWO: ACTUALIZATION

The Number Twenty-Two Name Number

The number twenty-two is similar to the number four. People with this number are often attracted to large movements or institutions that are aimed at the betterment and enlightenment of humanity. At their best, twenty-twos are capable of uniting people and forces to achieve their lofty aims. When negative, they can become greedy and lustful for power.

In their early years, twenty-twos may work in any number of menial and lowly positions in order to learn modesty and respect for those who will later work under their guidance and leadership.

The Number Twenty-Two Birthpath Number

Those with the twenty-two birthpath number have great powers of organization and are renowned for laying the solid foundations upon which great and powerful institutions are built: Although they may not lead the work, their contribution will be vital to its success.

Twenty-twos can become so engrossed in the labor of their missions that they can fail to recognize the human factor and the emotional needs of their coworkers. To succeed, they need to learn consideration, compassion, and humility.

It is essential that twenty-twos use their mental abilities in combined harmony with their bodies, emotions, and spirit. When thus disciplined, they become the master masons and builders of the world. Leonardo da Vinci, born on April 14, 1452, is a supreme example of an individual born with the twenty-two birthpath master number.

THIRTY-THREE: UNIVERSAL SERVICE

The Number Thirty-Three Name Number

Like the six, thirty-threes are highly attuned to the suffering of others and are subsequently drawn to institutions involved with health, education, research, and other humanitarian and philanthropic endeavors. Their overriding concerns are the relief of suffering and the betterment of mankind.

The Number Thirty-Three Birthpath Number

Those with the thirty-three birthpath have been born to serve mankind on a grand scale. Often, they must resolve their own deeply rooted and complex emotional issues before they can be of service to others. When negative, the thirty-three's self-righteousness and compulsion to help can be aggravating and self-defeating. When in harmony, and their emotional conflicts are resolved, they can become excellent healers, teachers, and counselors.

MORE

NUMEROLOGY

THE CONSONANTS:
YOUR PERSONA NUMBER

By adding together the numbers assigned to the consonants in your full birth name and reducing the sum to a single digit (with the exception of the master numbers eleven, twenty-two, and thirty-three), you arrive at what is known as your *persona number*. This is the number that shows the face or persona that enwraps you and that is your initial presentation to the outer world—how people first perceive you before they get to truly know who you really are. For an enhanced understanding of your persona number, refer to the explanations in the previous chapters on name and birthpath numbers.

The Number One Consonant

The resonance of the number one consonant is that of reserved self-possession, authority, and leadership. The number one also appears to radiate a certain nervous energy. In dress, the one consonant appears as fashionably tailored, with an air of quiet sophistication. They come across as confident, charming, and imperturbable. Their sense of personal dignity can even make them appear at first glance to be taller than they actually are.

The Number Two Consonant

The number two façade is that of gentility, reticence, and composure. Once introductions are properly made, however, shyness is overcome and the number two consonant is highly gregarious, a good talker and a good listener. The number two's aura of vulnerability and indecisiveness is likely initially to provoke the protective instincts of others, who soon discover that underneath the quiet and gentle manner of the two consonant lies an ability to meet any opposition with determined and convincing powers of persuasion.

The Number Three Consonant

The number three comes across as cheerful, humorous, entertaining, and highly sociable. Others may indeed think that the number three is incapable of ever being worried or depressed—a lighthearted bon vivant who regards the world as his oyster and sheds brightness, camaraderie, and gaiety wherever he goes.

The Number Four Consonant

Fours are perceived as solid, stable, disciplined, and conservative. They give the impression of being very pragmatic and secure, with fixed and definite attitudes, and able to give sound advice on practical matters such as mechanics, building, household repairs, and gardening, even if such things are actually of no interest to them.

The Number Five Consonant

Fives radiate strong sexual charisma. They have an aura of restless adventurism and wanderlust, both mentally and physically. They appear to be very quick on their feet, curious and open minded, adroit at improvisation and mingling freely and easily, keeping pace with the action and even being ahead of it. To some, the number five may appear as a person who could easily become bored and impatient and eager to move on if not sufficiently stimulated.

The Number Six Consonant

The image presented by the number six is that of empathy and kindness. People sense this immediately and are often more than ready to impart their woes, sensing an understanding, sincere, and compassionate listener who will offer comfort and advice. However, in spite of this congenial appearance, sixes will not allow others to force their opinions upon them and can become quite argumentative when challenged.

The Number Seven Consonant

Seven consonants appear as reserved and aloof, with an aura of mystery and illusion. They emit a strong sense of wisdom and self-knowledge. In conversation, they are probing and analytical, asking more questions than providing answers. They are refined, dignified, and aristocratic, and others are attracted by their air of chivalry and quiet intrigue.

The Number Eight Consonant

The immediate impression of an eight is that of success, prosperity, and executive ability. They come across as big thinkers and big talkers—as the "masters of the universe" in Tom Wolfe's *The Bonfire of the Vanities*. They are seen as organized, efficient, and usually very well tailored. Often secretive, it is not easy for them to be open or revealing about their personal lives, beliefs, and relationships. At times they appear to challenge and even embarrass others regarding their opinions or beliefs. This is not done out of malice, but merely to enliven conversation and test another's stamina and conviction. Eight consonants give off a strong impression of being in control both personally and professionally.

The Number Nine Consonant

The initial impression created by the nine consonant is one of worldly sophistication and enchanting magnetism. They appear as individuals who have been honed by a wide variety of experiences, although that may not actually be the case. They appear readily able to adapt to any situation, environment, or group. Their wardrobe is classic and artistic and often distinctly dark in shade—black, blue, purple, and dark brown, accented by hints of color.

The Number Eleven Consonant

Elevens radiate an energy that appears dynamic, vital, and kinetic. Their very presence can appear to light up a room, whether they are exuberantly engaging others or simply stepping back and quietly observing. Eleven consonants prefer to wear vibrant colors and smooth materials.

The Number Twenty-Two Consonant

Twenty-twos give off an aura of wealth, success, and expertise. They are perceived initially as being conservative and emotionally restrained yet generous, kind, and cooperative. Their clothing is simple and neat and carefully selected, as appearance is important to them.

The Number Thirty-Three Consonant

The impression here is one of congeniality, charm, dependability, and openness. However, he can also appear as high strung or extreme in his reactions when things don't go his way, and of being fickle mentally and emotionally—a person who seems to require or be attracted to a number of different lovers at the same time. Her wardrobe is highly stylish, and she can often appear as belonging to the social or cultural elite.

THE VOWELS:
YOUR SOUL NUMBER

By adding together the numbers assigned to the vowels in your full birth name and reducing them to a single digit (again, except for the master numbers eleven, twenty-two, and thirty-three), you arrive at your *soul number*, the number that describes your inner being, the forces that drive or motivate you, and your secret yearnings, aspirations, and goals. *Y* should be considered a vowel when it is the only vowel sound in a name or when it takes on the sound of the vowel preceding it, as in both vowels in the name *Sydney*.

The Number One Vowel

Number one vowels are driven by a strong need and desire to express themselves in individual and original ways, and to be Number One in both their careers and their personal lives. They are motivated by a sense of loyalty, honesty, and self-reliance, a desire to excel in whatever they do, to fearlessly meet and overcome new challenges, and to command the respect of others.

The Number Two Vowel

Two vowels are motivated by a strong inner desire for peace, partnership, and cooperation. They desire appreciation and support in all their ventures. They do not necessarily wish to lead, but to be essential instruments and part of a team effort in attaining a goal. Details are very important to them. They strive to achieve a romanticized ideal of love, peace, and harmony with their mates and associates.

The Number Three Vowel

Three vowels are motivated by imagination, creativity, optimism, and sociability. Friends and family are all important to them. They seek to express joy, hope, and beauty in everything they do, and to bring happiness to all. Theirs is a strong need to give and receive love.

The Number Four Vowel

Four vowels are driven by a strong desire for stability and security in their lives, in very concrete terms, and to be in control of their own lives and careers. They have little time for abstractions and theories, and care only for that which can be seen to render actual results in real and earthly terms. They show their affection in very practical ways, and desire stability and loyalty in love.

The Number Five Vowel

Five vowels are driven by a desire for freedom and worldly knowledge through experience. The five vowel feels a secret urge to overcome all restrictions and prejudices and to be athletic both physically and mentally—to be a magical being, free of all restrictions and able to defy the laws of gravity, leap tall buildings in a single bound, and fly over mountain ranges on winged horses in her hunger to consume all of life's wonders first hand. Five vowels are open minded and enthusiastic wanderers who seek to find meaning in new and interesting and bizarre people, places, and experiences, and who desire to bring the knowledge they acquire and their fascination for it to others. They want to demonstrate the true arcane meanings of freedom, tolerance, human variety, potential, inventiveness, eccentricity, progress, and the vividness and radiant magic of life in general. These men and women are disciples of the strange and are children of the world, and often are its magicians, as they seek knowledge through the senses and so understand the sensory "veil of illusion," the invisible meaning that lies behind all that is visible, or in Pythagorean terms, the "Limited" that gives form to the "Unlimited." Marco Polo was in many ways a prototypical five. Friendship and freedom in devotion without possessiveness is what a five seeks most in a lover.

The Number Six Vowel

Six vowels are motivated by a desire to serve and protect others, as well as to provide the best life has to offer for both themselves and their loved ones. They are driven by a strong humanitarian concern for justice, equality, fairness, and sustenance for all, sometimes with missionary zeal, and are truly empathetic to the suffering of others.

The Number Seven Vowel

Intellectual pursuits, the life of the mind, analysis, and meticulous investigation in the search for knowledge and truth are at the key motivations for the number seven vowel. "Why is it so?" is the question that drives them. Although very romantic, gentle, and caring, they have little time for the emotional aspects of relationships, and prefer lovers who share their intellectual curiosity, detachment, objectivity, and rational inquiry of life and its mysteries.

The Number Eight Vowel

Ambition, the desire for power and success, is the key motivator for the number eight vowel. They seek the authority to organize and manage the affairs of others. They are disciplined and straightforward in their approach. In love they can appear to be unemotional and even businesslike, but they are responsible and loyal. When positive, they strive for a balance between the spiritual and material and are fair and ethical in their business dealings.

The Number Nine Vowel

Nine vowels are motivated by their ideals and dreams. Like the number six, they have a strong desire to be of service, but more as teacher and visionary. They are seekers of perfection, universal understanding, tolerance, progress, and harmony. In their idealism they are inclined to more readily perceive the world as it ought to be rather than for what it is. They desire the perfect lover and companion, and in relationships can be blinded by emotion. They are motivated by contact with other people, and will not tolerate a mate who limits them socially.

The Number Eleven Vowel

Eleven vowels are motivated by a zealous need to bring inventive ideas to reality. They inspire those around them to action through their enthusiasm, faith, and idealism. They are emotionally sensitive and highly romantic, and are lovers of the arts, as well as of peace, cooperation, and harmony. They deplore conflict, and have great gifts of subtle persuasion, recognizing the value of diplomacy as a means of achieving their goals.

The Number Twenty-Two Vowel

Twenty-two vowels blend the idealism of the eleven with the practical discipline of the four, making them inspired dreamers and builders. They desire to be the rock upon which others can lean and great structures can be built. They seek to provide strength, security, and stability through their friendships and association with others. Once they have mastered their own abilities, no feat seems too large to accomplish. They wish to be the grand schemers and of great undertakings that bring concrete benefit to humanity at large.

The Number Thirty-Three Vowel

Thirty-three vowels are driven by high-minded altruism, principals, and humanistic ideals. They possess a great understanding of humanity and its needs, and are capable of seeing goodness where others may see none, inspiring those around them to perform acts of kindness and mercy rather cruelty or indifference.

YOUR PERSONAL YEAR NUMBER

Your personal year number helps you forecast what the current year holds in store for you and can help you recognize the most appropriate time to enter a new relationship, shift careers, move your home, and make other life changes. You can find your personal year number by adding the numbers of your month of birth, your day of birth, and the current calendar year, again, including all four digits of the year: 1962, not '62.

The personal years repeat in nine-year cycles. Each time the cycle is renewed, it provides the individual with an opportunity for self-renewal, growth, and new beginnings. Each nine-year cycle is replete with chances for increasing self-knowledge and worldly wisdom. If these opportunities are resisted or ignored, or are not met because of sloth, indifference, or cynicism, the same situations or very similar ones will reoccur.

The Number One Personal Year

The one personal year begins a new cycle of nine years. It is the time to convert ideas, dreams, and aspirations into direct and meaningful action. This year offers new opportunities in life, love, and career. It is a year to fearlessly take on the world, to seize the day without doubt or hesitation, and to face and overcome any unconscious blockages, conflicts, and fears that have hindered and thwarted you in the past. This is the time for the introspection that brings clarity and self-knowledge combined with correct and decisive external action.

The early months of the one year tend to be given over to the laying of new foundations, followed by potential opportunities for expansion and breakthrough. The middle months are for introspection, assessment, the implementation of new goals, and the shedding of habits and attitudes that are no longer appropriate. Toward the end of the year, new opportunities start to present themselves clearly.

In the one personal year, new relationships tend to start up, or ties to existing ones are renewed and strengthened on a higher plane, including marriage. It is a time when lovers become best friends, and best friends lovers. It is also a time in which floundering or static relationships can end, clearing the path for new opportunities.

The Number Two Personal Year

This is the time to nurture and foster that which was sown in the number one year. New ideas and opportunities that presented themselves in the previous year should now start to bear fruit. If resistance, opposition, or indifference occurred in the previous year, you should be prepared for difficulties and emotional trials that force you to release psychological and emotional blockages and move you into a deeper understanding of yourself and your circumstances. Understanding of others and cooperation are the keys to your success this year. This is a year in which you are to receive and share rather than to aggressively push and assert.

If you welcome and embrace the opportunities this year offers, you may be able to recognize and attract the mate most suitable for you.

The Number Three Personal Year

This is a year of creativity, new ideas, and self-expression. It is also a year in which hidden fears and guilt concerning sexual matters can come to the fore. It is a good year for making new friends and business contacts. Those who are single have a strong likelihood of being active with a love partner. However, it is not necessarily a good time to fall in love, as you run the risk of falling in love with love itself rather than with the right person.

The three year tends to start off very businesslike. It is a good time to take note of inspired thoughts and ideas that may very well pay off later. The early months of the year will provide many new and intriguing social contacts. Mid-year is a time for meditation and organization, followed by a time for friendships, enjoyment, and creative breakthrough. It is also a time in which you may very well attract a potential marriage partner.

The Number Four Personal Year

Work, business, career, and security are the hallmarks of the four personal year. It is the time to build a solid foundation for your life's work, and many opportunities will present themselves to enhance your efforts. It could very well bring you the chance to do that one thing you've been wanting to do all of your life. If you feel discontent or are stuck in a rut in your career, it is a good year to change your direction.

The year may start off with such a flourish of activity that it seems you'll have everything you desire by the year's end. However, things tend to fall apart on the emotional and personal side of your life during the next four months. Do not allow this to affect your work performance. From mid-year on, important new opportunities and developments start to present themselves.

The Number Five Personal Year

This is a year for growth, change, freedom, and enjoyment. It is a year for travel and discovery, both mental and physical. New friends are made, and perhaps you'll move into a new residence or even to a new city or country. Intuition and curiosity are given free rein, and new lessons can be learned. Impulsiveness, restlessness, and impatience are also part of this year. The sexual and sensual are accentuated, bringing dangerous temptations along with good times. There is a strong need to break with the past.

The year begins with a strong and restless urge for change. This could cause tension in relationships and marriage. Summer will be exciting and adventurous. New doors will open, new relationships formed, and new paths and opportunities discovered.

The Number Six Personal Year

The focus of this year is on service, responsibility to others, marriage, sacrifice, and the resolution of personal conflicts. The year offers little in terms of satisfying personal desires. It is a year to give more than to take, a year in which altruism is tested. If there is underlying tension in a marriage or relationship, it will become aggravated if it is not resolved. The marriage or affair will either end or be reborn on a deeper level of mutual cooperation. If single, there is a strong desire for companionship, marriage, and family. Quite likely, someone you met or were involved with during the adventurous and frantic five year will reemerge as a potential mate.

The first three months could see delays in your plans and business affairs. It is a time to reexamine your motives and intentions. Activity will increase mid-year, with the demands of personal responsibilities reaching a peak by the year's end. A troubled relationship could fall apart during the last months of the year, while relationships that are more firmly based will deepen and mature in tenderness and consideration.

The Number Seven Personal Year

This is a year for meditation, introspection, and self-examination. It is a lonely year in many respects, but loneliness has its place. This year promotes philosophical searching and intellectual investigation. Illumination can come from within. Unique and unusual ties can be formed with those who share your interests. It is not a time for marriage. A seven personal year can mean separation. It is best to let existing relationships stand the test of time during this period. If it is meant to be, then it will be.

The Number Eight Personal Year

This is a year marked by advancement, increased social status, power, authority, executive ability, and money. It is important, however, to proceed slowly and cautiously. Often, the rewards of the eight year have been your just due for quite some time, and you may feel some underlying resentment. When recognition does come, it is important that you do not succumb to false pride and brashness. Money pursued merely for power and greed may easily slip through your fingers. Money acquired through productivity will grow and bring even greater dividends. Also be wary of confrontation. It is a time to be flexible and willing to learn from others.

This is a good year to attract a partner. If in a relationship or marriage, existing ties can be strengthened and solidified.

The Number Nine Personal Year

This is the end of the cycle, bringing one period of life to a close while offering the prospect of renewal. Nine is inclusive of all the other numbers, so this year is marked by a wide variety of experiences, opportunities, and events. Generally, it is not the time to marry or embark on a new business venture. This can be the easiest time to let go of old psychological and emotional burdens and negative feelings and attitudes. It is time to let go of the past in order to prepare for the new cycle that is about to begin, and those who insist on clinging to it will have a difficult year. For those who are able to purge themselves, the last three months of the year will bring a marvelous sense of freedom, awakening, and enjoyment.

The Number Eleven Personal Year

The eleven personal year is in many ways similar to the two. This year brings inspired thinking, originality, and invention. You can gain prominence or influential position. Sudden or unexpected associations and affairs, along with potential breakups, are possible.

The Number Twenty-Two Personal Year

The twenty-two personal year is very similar to the four. Opportunities to both serve and lay foundations will present themselves on a grand scale.

The Number Thirty-Three Personal Year

The thirty-three personal year is much like the six. Difficult sacrifices may be required. It is a time to meet the needs of others and learn to give of yourself. It is especially a year for developing special platonic relationships.

THE PINNACLES

The pinnacles represent the four stages, or cycles of change and development, that we pass through in our lives. The pinnacles are preordained by our birth dates. Knowing them can reveal the nature of what lies ahead for us on our life journey and help prepare us for things to come.

The First and Fourth Pinnacles last for thirty years (or more, as in the case of the Fourth Pinnacle) while the Second and Third Pinnacles are both nine years long.

To calculate your number of the First Pinnacle, add together only the day and the month of birth, and reduce it to a single digit.

To calculate your number of the Second Pinnacle, add together the day and year of birth and reduce to a single digit.

To calculate your number of the Third Pinnacle, add the numbers of the First and Second Pinnacles together, and reduce it to a single digit.

To calculate your number of the Fourth Pinnacle—the Major Pinnacle—add the month and year of birth and reduce it to a single digit.

As explained previously, all numbers are reduced to a single digit except for the master numbers eleven, twenty-two, and thirty-three.

Once you have calculated your pinnacle numbers, you should read the chapters on the equivalent birthpath numbers, and descriptions of the personal year numbers. These will inform you of the basic themes of each of the pinnacles.

THE CHALLENGE NUMBERS

Challenge numbers represent those personal obstacles, emotional blockages, and character traits that we must recognize and overcome if we are to grow and prosper and live up to our full potential. There are four life challenges contained within the numbers of your birth date. The most important is called the Major Challenge, which will remain with you throughout your entire life. The other three Minor Challenges appear for shorter periods of time and are linked to the Major Challenge.

The First Minor Challenge affects the first twenty-eight years of life, generally corresponding to the First Pinnacle (which covers the first thirty years). To find the number of the First Minor Challenge, reduce the numbers for the month and day of birth to single digits, then subtract the smaller number from the larger. This number represents the First Minor Challenge.

The Second Minor Challenge is active from the ages of twenty-eight to approximately fifty-six, and is most active during the transit into the Second Pinnacle (which begins, as noted earlier, at age thirty). To find the number of the Second Minor Challenge, reduce the numbers for the day and year of birth to single digits and subtract the smaller from the larger. This is the number of the Second Minor Challenge.

The Third Minor Challenge is in effect from the age of fifty-six onward, and is particularly strong during the transit into the Fourth Pinnacle. It is found by reducing the numbers of the month and the year of birth to single digits and then subtracting the smaller number from the larger.

The Major Challenge is active for our entire lives, from birth to death. Its number is found by subtracting the First Minor Challenge and the Second Minor Challenge, naturally, the smaller number from the larger.

The Number One Challenge

The challenge here is to face the responsibilities of leadership and to find the correct balance between ego and cooperation. It warns against being overly egotistical, willful, stubborn, and selfish, and encourages learning compassion, consideration, and understanding of others.

The Number Two Challenge

The challenge of the number two is to overcome lack of confidence and belief in one's own abilities. It warns against indecisiveness and vacillation, oversensitivity to criticism, and lack of courage to take initiative.

The Number Three Challenge

The number three warns against lack of self-worth (as distinguished from self-confidence) and squandering one's talents and creative abilities. It cautions you to embrace personal discipline and bring ideas to practical fruition and to complete what you start.

The Number Four Challenge

The challenge here is to overcome laziness, inflexibility, lack of imagination, and fear of change. It cautions against imposing too many restrictions upon both oneself and others. It also is a challenge to find the means to lay a solid foundation and find stability and security in life, and urges logical planning of goals and finances to ensure success.

The Number Five Challenge

The number five cautions against the abuse of human freedom, overindulgence of the senses, and reckless abandon both morally and physically. It also demands that any fear of change or of taking risks, any personal and social timidity, and nervousness be overcome.

The Number Six Challenge

This is a challenge of responsibility, service, acceptance, and adjustment. Its lesson is to learn the value of selflessness and altruism while maintaining a healthy and protected sense of the self, of how to give and care for others while at the same time not being taken advantage of. Often, it means that a self-centered and selfish individual must learn these things to attain the love and union with another that they secretly yearn for. It also warns against being overly possessive and interfering, and expecting too much from others in return.

The Number Seven Challenge

This is a challenge to look deeper into the meaning of life's experiences, to bring intuitive as well as mental powers to bear, and to find the balance between the two. It cautions against being overly analytical and intellectual, and promotes the awareness of intuitive abilities as a means to knowledge and understanding.

The Number Eight Challenge

This is a very basic challenge of values and judgment—both spiritual and material. The number eight is concerned with the acquiring and handling of power and money, and with correct motivation. It represents a test of moral values and keen insight and acumen. Materialism, the superficial drive for power and wealth for their own sakes, needs to be overcome; otherwise the individual will be burdened with opposition and loss. It is a challenge to learn both the source and true meaning and value of power, authority, and success.

The Number Zero Challenge Number

No number nine challenge exists in numerology. The nine and the zero are the same. They represent the death of the old, the rebirth of the new, and the space in between—the hiatus and interregnum between transitions.

The zero challenge, like the nine, is a combination and variety of all the numbers. It could mean that there are several challenges or none at all. Those with the zero challenge are destined to have a wide variety of experiences and associations from which they will learn and discern. The zero has the remarkable choice of either self-motivated, independent action and personal destiny, or attaching themselves to and aiding another, to ride with them on their chariot into the arena of success. The choice is the number zero's.

COMPATIBILITY
IN RELATIONSHIPS

The following is a simple listing of compatibility between the numbers.

One

Especially good with the independent and adventurous five; also good with one, two, and three; eight when authority and leadership are not in competition; seven and nine in special circumstances.

Two, Eleven

Good with one, four, six, and eight; attracted to five, who may be very exciting but too restless and busy.

Three

Good with one, three, five, six, and nine; seven and eight under special circumstances; four or twenty-two can be good as stabilizers for the three, but may at times be too practical and set in their ways.

Four, Twenty-Two

Usually good with one, two, six, and seven; sometimes three and eight; four with four share similar concerns but may end up stuck in a rut together.

Five

Especially good with the independent one and the imaginative nine. Sometimes compatible with three, six, seven, and eight.

Six, Thirty-Three

Good with two, three, four, six, and eight; one can be good if it is not too self-centered and independent; attracted to five, who may be too unpredictable and freedom-loving; nine can make a good match.

Seven

Good with four, five, seven; one and nine in special cases; three and seven can have magical moments together but may not last.

Eight

Usually good with one and four if neither person is stubborn or competitive; two, three, five, and six also good; nine in special cases.

Nine

Can be good with three, five, six, seven, or another nine; four is loyal and a stabilizing influence, and this combination can work under special circumstances.

FURTHER READING

Burket, Walter. *Lore and Science in Ancient Pythagoreanism.* Cambridge, MA: Harvard University Press, 1972.

Campbell, Florence. *Your Days Are Numbered.* Ferndale, PA: Gateway, 1975.

Casanova, Giacomo. *Casanova's Book of Numbers and Daily Astrology.* Seattle, WA: Vulcan Books, 1975.

Cheiro. *The Cheiro Book of Fate and Fortune: Palmistry, Numerology, Astrology.* New York: Arco Publishing Co., 1971.

Decoz, Hans. *Numerology: The Key To Your Inner Self.* New York: Avery Publishing Group, 1994.

Johnson, Vera Scott. *The Secrets of Numbers: A Numerological Guide to Your Character and Destiny.* New York: Dial Press, 1973.

Leek, Sybil. *Numerology: The Magic of Numbers.* New York: Collier Books, 1969.

Shine, Norman. *Numerology: Your Character and Future Revealed in Numbers.* New York: Simon and Schuster, 1994.

ABOUT THE AUTHOR

Damian Sharp was born in Australia and resides in San Francisco. He is the recipient of two Literary Fellowship Awards from the Australian Council for the Arts. He is the author of *Simple Feng Shui* and *Simple Chinese Astrology* and has written several short stories, including a collection entitled *When a Monkey Speaks*. He is currently at work on a second book of short stories.

A Simple Wisdom Book

Simple Numerology is part of Conari Press' A Simple Wisdom Book series which seeks to provide accessible books on enlightening topics.

Other titles in the Simple Wisdom Book series:

Simple Meditation & Relaxation
by Joel Levey and Michelle Levey

Simple Feng Shui by Damian Sharp

Simple Kabbalah by Kim Zetter

Simple Chinese Astrology by Damian Sharp

Simple Yoga by Cybèle Tomlinson

Simple Wicca by Michele Morgan

CONARI PRESS

2550 Ninth Street, Suite 101
Berkeley, California 94710-2551
800-685-9595   510-649-7175
fax: 510-649-7190   e-mail: conari@conari.com
http://www.conari.com